Humpty Dumpty sat on a wall.
Humpty Dumpty had a great fall.
All the king's horses and all the king's men
Couldn't put Humpty together again.

Traditional nursery rhyme

Everyone knows the story of Humpty Dumpty.
Not so many know the story of his little sister, Dimity.
Now her story can be told...

Dimity Dumpty was born by the roadside.
She cried a small note in perfect tune with
a blackbird singing outside her window.
"It's a girl!" cried her mum and dad, overjoyed.
Humpty did a cartwheel and two double twists.

Specially for Oscar, Lucy and David

First published 2006 by Walker Books Ltd
87 Vauxhall Walk, London, SE11 5HJ

10 9 8 7 6 5 4 3 2 1

© 2006 Blackbird Design Pty. Ltd.

The right of Bob Graham to be identified as author/illustrator of this work has
been asserted by him in accordance with the Copyright, Designs and Patents Act 1988

This book has been typeset in BodonAntiqua Reg

Printed in China

British Library Cataloguing in Publication Data:
a catalogue record for this book is available from the British Library

ISBN-13: 978-1-84428-067-4
ISBN-10: 1-84428-067-5

www.walkerbooks.co.uk

DIMITY DUMPTY

The Story of Humpty's Little Sister

Bob Graham

WALKER BOOKS
AND SUBSIDIARIES
LONDON · BOSTON · SYDNEY · AUCKLAND

The Dumpty family were part of a travelling circus.
Along many roads they bumped: down icy winter highways and
up summer country lanes, from town to town.
As he grew, Humpty turned into something of a tearaway.

"Sit down, Humpty," his mum often said to him.

"One of these days you'll come a cropper."

Dimity grew too. Unlike her brother, she was shy and timid as a fieldmouse.

Her small voice lost itself in the noise of the wheels and the dust of the road.

But it was in the dust of the road that one day a gift lay waiting for her.

It was Dimity's father, Dominic, who found the old pen.

He removed the case and, from the inside,
made his daughter a little silver flute.

Dimity's first notes were soft as the breeze itself.

There was always much
to do when the circus
came to town:

the hen to be fed
and watered,

ropes to be pulled, pegs to be hammered in, the Big Top to go up...

And there were shows to be performed.
Dimity watched as her family applied the paint,
dusted their hands and became ...

THE TUMBLING DUMPTIES.

"Won't you join us, honey?"
asked her mum, Dorothy, before each show.
Every time, Dimity shook her head.
"No, thank you," she replied.

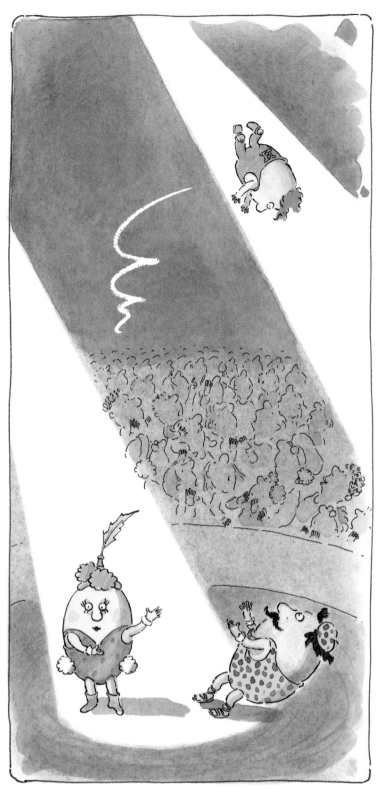

At showtime, the Tumbling
Dumpties brought the circus
crowd to its feet with
breathtaking displays of danger.

The Great Dominic Dumpty threw
his son, Humpty, high in the air.
Humpty turned, end over end, the
circus lights glinting on his fragile shell.

Then Dorothy and Dominic Dumpty flew from the trapeze, high in the roof of the circus tent. To Dimity in the shadows below, her mother looked beautiful, transformed like a butterfly – but as the crowd roared and the spotlight pushed like a bright finger across the tent ...

she would look for a quieter place.

Up above the circus ground,
she blew into her silver flute –
soft as a snail on a cabbage leaf,
quiet as the grass growing on the hill,
gentle as a beetle's breath,
making sounds known only to birds
and things that slide in the night.

No light had ever caught Dimity
in its bright glare.

One hot summer day, when Humpty's tumble was over and their
parents were still spinning and turning in the top of the tent,
Humpty and Dimity opened the roof of the caravan.

Dimity's fingers found a little cool tune on her flute.
Humpty's fingers found his mum's lipstick.
"That's not too clever, Humpty," gasped Dimity, when she saw
what he was doing, "to write your name on your own wall."

When their parents returned from the spotlight, moisture still drying on their
hot shells, Dominic's foot tapped and Dorothy's finger quivered.

"Clean it off right now, Humpty," said his mum,

"or trouble will come knocking at your door."

And trouble did come calling the following afternoon when Humpty,
once more with time on his hands, found a spray can by the old factory wall.

Yes, trouble arrived, along with the storm clouds brewing over the town.
Humpty climbed on to the wall, sprayed his name ... and slipped.

Passing soldiers and their horses were no help at all.

"It's only an egg," said one soldier to another,

and they returned to their barracks.

Only an egg?

Only an egg!

This egg (however naughty with a spray can) was someone's brother.

That Humpty had a great fall is known well enough.
What is not known is the courage of his little sister.

Far away on the other side of the circus, Dimity heard
a tremor in the wind and felt a flutter right down
deep in her little shell.

She picked up her skirts and ran.

Dimity stopped. Her hands went to her face.
She took a deep breath ...

then removed her T-shirt

and bandaged Humpty's leakage.

She laid her little flute along
Humpty's leg and wrapped
her skirt around it.

She tried to stop passers by.
"Please help my brother!"
she called.
But nobody heard her.

There was only one thing to do...

Once more, she ran.

Dimity reached the tent, slowly lifted the flap ...

and found her voice.

"MY BROTHER HAS TAKEN
A TUMBLE AND NEEDS HELP!"

And help came immediately, with Dimity leading the way to rescue Humpty.

In hospital, Humpty received lots of visitors and lots of chocolates.

Even the soldiers came when they heard it on the radio.

"We are sorry, Humpty. What can we do to make up for this?" they asked.

"A ride on your horse when I get out?" asked Humpty, at once.

"A big cheer for Dimity, and as many of her
brother's chocolates as she can eat!" said a clown.
Somewhere down behind her mother's skirts,
Dimity blushed.

Dimity is still shy and timid as a fieldmouse.

She has never returned to the spotlight,
nor joined the Tumbling Dumpties.
But she *has* changed, and there has been
a change around the circus, too.

In the mornings, when the bright lights
from last night's show are only a memory,
Dimity's silver flute can be heard in the
sunlight and shadows of the circus grounds.

The music slips under doorways,
through skylights and windows ...
as surely and pleasantly
as the smell of hot chocolate.

The high notes fly like swifts on
a summer's morning and the low notes
whisper like wind in the pine trees,
but Dimity's tunes can still be heard
right across the circus ground.
They sparkle like the sun on the water.

"It's the music of the heavens," says the
ringmaster. "Let the tent come down,
but all in good time."

Only when she can play no more does the tent
come down – until the next stop and the next show
somewhere down the road.

As for Humpty,

he made a full recovery

and has put away his spray can.

He is now on the trapeze with the

Tumbling Dumpties and rides the

soldier's horse in an act

of his own.